Toulmin Smith

The Right Holding of the Coroner's Court

Anatiposi

Toulmin Smith

The Right Holding of the Coroner's Court

Reprint of the original.

1st Edition 2023 | ISBN: 978-3-38230-522-2

Anatiposi Verlag is an imprint of Outlook Verlagsgesellschaft mbH.

Verlag (Publisher): Outlook Verlag GmbH, Zeilweg 44, 60439 Frankfurt, Deutschland
Vertretungsberechtigt (Authorized to represent): E. Roepke, Zeilweg 44, 60439 Frankfurt, Deutschland
Druck (Print): Books on Demand GmbH, In de Tarpen 42, 22848 Norderstedt, Deutschland

THE RIGHT HOLDING

OF

THE CORONER'S COURT;

AND

Some recent Interferences therewith:

BEING

A REPORT

Laid before the ROYAL COMMISSIONERS *appointed to inquire into*
" *The Law now regulating the Payment of the Expenses*
of holding Coroners' Inquests."

BY

TOULMIN SMITH,

OF LINCOLN'S INN, ESQ., BARRISTER-AT-LAW.

LONDON:
HENRY SWEET, 3, CHANCERY LANE.
1859.

THE RIGHT HOLDING

OF

THE CORONER'S COURT.

———◆———

1. The "Law regulating the payment of the expenses of holding Coroners' Inquests," is a matter which, whatever interest
Coroners themselves may have in it, concerns the Public in a
far greater degree. To the Coroners, looking at it as a personal question, it is merely a matter of a few pounds, more or
less. To the Public, it is a matter of maintaining the safeguards of human life.

2. The only way in which this Law can be truly known, is
by tracing its history. It is thus only that the spirit and
principle of the Law on any subject whatever can be really
understood; and it is because this course has not been taken
in dealing with some late cases that have arisen touching Coroners' Inquests, that any doubt has been able to be raised as
to the construction of a particular Statute,—that of 25 Geo.
II. c. 29. It is from the want of knowledge thus existing,
and exhibited, that difficulties have been able to be raised, by
a few Justices of the Peace, in the way of the right exercise of
the functions of Coroners.

3. The only way in which any Statute can be rightly interpreted, and have force given to it by the Courts of Law,
was laid down with clearness and unevadible logical pre-
ciseness in Heydon's Case (Lord Coke's Reports, iii. 7 (*h*)).

It was there resolved by the whole Court, "that, for the sure and true interpretation of all Statutes in general (be they penal or beneficial, restrictive or enlarging of the Common Law), four things are to be discerned and considered;—

"(1.) What was the Common Law before the making of the Act.

'(2.) What was the mischief and defect for which the Common Law did not provide.

"(3.) What remedy the parliament hath resolved and appointed to cure the disease of the Commonwealth.

"(4.) The true reason of the remedy.

"And then the Office of all the judges is always to make such construction as shall *suppress the mischief, and advance the remedy;* and to *suppress subtle inventions and evasions for continuance of the mischief, and to add force and life to the cure and remedy,* according to the true intent of the makers of the Act." (See the same words in Magdalen College Case, xi. Co. Rep. 73 (*b*); and compare i. Rep. 123 (*a*).)

4. In another place, Lord Coke repeats that, "Construction must be made of a Statute, in suppression of the mischief, and in advancement of the remedy" (Coke on Littleton, 381 (*b*));—the nature of the "mischief" being only able to be learned by the History of the subject, as he always, and wisely, insists on.

5. Inquisitions upon the Death of Man, and the Coroner's Court for taking these,—unlike Justices of the Peace, who are the mere creation of Statutes, and whose powers are therefore limited by the express letter of Statute Law,—derive neither their origin nor their authority from any Statute. They have their roots in the Common Law; and Statute Law has only been applied to what touches them, with the object of not letting the requisitions of the Common Law fall into forgetfulness, but of ensuring that this Institution shall be kept in full and unremitting independent activity. Hence, the key to the true interpretation of any modern Statutes on the subject, can only be found by learning what is the Common Law in regard to the same matter. Happily, we are

not left in any doubt as to this. The Law relating to Coroners has come down to us from a time earlier than any Statute that exists upon the subject.

6. Bracton's treatise on the Laws of England was written in the time of Henry III.; several years earlier, therefore, than the earliest Statutes touching the Coroners' Inquisition. He describes " Homicide in fact " as of four kinds; namely, " by *justice, necessity, chance*, and *will*." The first case is that which arises in the course of the administration of the Law. The second is that which is inevitable for self-defence. The third, —" chance," or " misadventure,"—is described to be " when any one has cast a stone at a bird or animal, and one passing by is unexpectedly struck and killed; *or* if any one has felled a tree, and any one has been killed by the fall of it; and cases of the like sort. But here it must be noted whether one has been doing what is lawful or unlawful. If unlawful,—as if one had cast a stone towards a place along which men were accustomed to go and come; or if, while one follows a horse or an ox, some one has been struck by the ox or the horse; and the like,—this shall be ground of charge. If lawful,—as if a master shall strike his pupil; or if one shall put a load of hay out of a cart, or shall fell a tree, or the like; if he have shown as much care as he could,—for instance, by giving forewarning in proper time, and so that any one might avoid danger, and if the master has not overpassed moderation in his blow,—this shall not be ground of charge. But even a lawful thing, done without due care, will be ground of charge." The fourth kind of homicide, " by will," is ordinary murder. (Bracton, De Legibus, lib. iii. c. 4.)

7. Bracton goes on to describe what the function of the Coroner is in every one of these cases of homicide. " Whether it be in a house, or in a town, or in a hamlet, or in a common outside a town, or in a wood, it behoves the Coroner to get knowledge as to the slain; and if the slayer be unknown, to make diligent inquiry as to him. Hence it is right to state here what is his function. It is, then, the Coroner's duty that, as soon as he shall receive Notice from a bailiff [elected

local officer] or from honest men of the neighbourhood, he must go to whoever has been thus killed or wounded, or drowned, or suddenly dead, and to house-breakings, and to any place where treasure is said to have been found;—*and this must be done immediately, and without any delay.* And upon his arrival there, he must summon the four, five, or six neighbouring parishes, that they immediately come before him; and these shall make inquiry upon oath, touching the dead man, when they have been called on by the Coroner. In the first place, whether he have died in a house or in a field: then, whether at a quarrel, or at a tavern, or other crowd. And *wheresoever a dead man shall have been found,* it shall be inquired who were then present, male and female, elder and younger, and who among them were implicated in the deed, whether by force, advice, or command, and who were anywise concerned therein. . . . And if any be *drowned,* or *suddenly dead,* or *killed* by *violence,* or by *any misadventure,* INQUISITION MUST BE MADE IN THE SAME MANNER; and the bodies of the dead must be seen, naked and uncovered, howsoever they may have died, so that it may be known *whether* it be felony OR *misadventure,* so far as the outward marks show it." (Bracton, lib. iii. c. 5.)

8. Horne wrote in the next reign. He declares it to be the duty of the Coroner to view the bodies of those who have died, whether " by felony or by mischance ;" and to view *arsons,* etc. He gives the points of inquiry, which the Coroner is bound to set before the Jury. " You shall say, upon your oaths, as to the death of this man, *whether* he died by felony *or by mischance.* If by felony, whether by his own or another's. If by accident, *whether it has befallen of God or of man.* If by hunger, *whether through poverty or through a common pestilence.* . . . Whether he died of long imprisonment, or of punishment; and through whose means he became *less likely to live and more likely to die.* And so of all the circumstances that can weigh as means of judgment." (Horne: Mirrour, ch. i. § 13: and see pars. 9, 61.)

9. Fleta, written in the same reign, after declaring the

duty of the Coroner to hold inquiry in every case of murder
and homicide (lib. i. cap. 18), divides homicide, as Bracton had
done before him, into homicide by justice, by necessity, by
accident, and by will. The author goes on to state the course
of the Coroner's proceeding, in a manner no less clear than
Bracton. "When," he says, "a homicide has been com-
mitted, or an *accident* of this sort has happened, the *neighbours* shall tell it to the nearest Coroner; who, as soon as he
has notice, ought to come to the man that has been wounded
[killed by wounds], or drowned, or suddenly died. . . . The
bodies of those drowned, or suddenly dead, or by violence, or
by accident, or in any other manner, must be seen naked, so
that it can be seen *whether* they have died through felony or
accident: and *if it shall be deemed accident, then the manner
of it must be inquired.*" (ib. cap. 25.) This writer adds :—
"When prisoners die, they must not be buried before they
have been seen by the Coroner, and diligent inquest has been
held as to the manner of their deaths; for it sometimes happens
that those who have been imprisoned, die rather through unjust
punishment than by a natural death; and in that case their
keepers are to be deemed guilty of homicide." (ib. cap. 26.)

10. Britton, another and equally distinguished of the same
group of writers, after describing the Coroners, as all writers
do, as "the chief *Wardens* of the peace in each county,"
says that "no felony *nor misadventure* shall happen, nor man
drowned, *nor other mischance*, but the Coroner shall, as soon
as he knows it, command the sheriff, or the constable of the
place where the thing has happened, that, on a day named, he
cause to come before him, at the place where it happened, the
four next towns, and others if need were; *by whom* he shall
inquire the truth of the thing. And when they are come,
he shall make the towns swear that they will say the truth
as to the matters which he shall put before them." (Britton,
ed. 1640, p. 3 (*b*).) "And then let the Coroner go, and the jurors
with him, to view the bodies, and the wounds, and the hurts,
or if any be strangled, or smothered, or put to death by other
violence. And presently after the view, the bodies shall be

buried. And if the coroner find the bodies buried before such view be made, he shall cause that fact to be entered on his roll. But the coroner, nevertheless, shall not omit that he cause the bodies to be dug up and plainly viewed by the jury. . . . And the coroner shall make inquisition, quite from the beginning, *whether* such a man were killed by felony *or* by *misaventure*. And if the coroner has any suspicion that, at the first inquest, there has been any concealment of the truth, or that it would be better further to inquire and by others, he shall hold inquest again." (ib. p. 4 (*b*).) "And if it is found that any is dead by *misadventure*, then it must be inquired by *what misadventure;* if he was drowned, or fallen down, or killed without any felonious purpose, or felo-de-se; and if drowned, whether in the sea or in fresh-water, or in a well, or in a ditch, and by what cause he was drowned, and from what vessel he fell, etc. And if it shall be in a well, then it shall be inquired to whom the well belongs. And if it have been a fall, whether from a mill, or a horse, or a house, or a tree." (ib. p. 6.) A little further on, the same writer more carefully describes the misadventures which thus require an Inquest; and distinguishes what other writers have all included under the one name, sometimes of "aventure," and at other times of "misadventure," into two groups, though under one heading. "*Aventure*," he says, "is when death comes to a man without felony; as when one *suddenly dies by any sudden malady*, or falls in the fire, or in the water, and remains so long that he is quite dead: and *misadventure* [mesaventure] is if one dies by a fall from a tree, a ship, a gate, a cart, a horse, a mill, or other like cases, where no felony is done. In these cases [inasmuch as the inquest discloses no criminal deed], there is no need to levy the hue and cry, nor that presentment be made of the parent nor of the towns at the next County Court: *but the Coroner's Inquest will be enough*" (ib. cap. 7, p. 15 (*b*)). (See after, par. 15.)

11. The language thus used by these different masters in the Common Law, is so precise, and, though differing, so unequivocal and mutually illustrative, that it leaves nothing to be

desired, in proof of "what was the Common Law before the making of the Acts" on this subject. It will be seen that, through all, the chief stress is laid upon the necessity of an inquest being held in every case of "Misadventure." It will be found that the entire course of Statute Law has been to enforce the same thing.

12. Before recalling the Statute Law, it should be remarked that the Office of Coroner has not only always been that of Conservator of the Peace, the chief Conservator of the Peace in the Shire next to the Sheriff, but that it has always been one of greater judicial trust and credit than even that of the Sheriff himself. The highest judicial functions in the County Court have always been lodged in the Coroner, not in the Sheriff. It is very remarkable that, in the "*Articuli Magnæ Chartæ*," it is specifically laid down that "No sheriff shall deal with [intromittat] pleas of the crown *without the Coroners.*" And in a document two hundred years later, it is recited that whereas Assizes cannot be held without the presence of the Coroner, and it is sometimes difficult to ensure his attendance at the Assizes within the City of London ; and the Sheriffs are then empowered to hold the Assizes there, though the Coroner fails to attend ; "provided," the enactment concludes, "that this shall not be in derogation of the Office of the Coroner." (Rolls of Parliament, 1 Hen. IV. 89.) In the Statute of Merton, Coroners have the special title given to them of "Guardians of the Pleas of the Crown" (and see Second Institute, p. 84). At the present day, the judgments in Outlawry are given, not by the Sheriff, but by the Coroners of the County. In all records, the act or declaration of the Coroner carries the highest weight, and he can do many things that no Justice can do ; the reason for which, assigned by Lord Coke himself, is, "because the Coroners are chosen by the whole County,"—a reason and fact which are as sound and true at this day as they have ever been. (See Coke's Reports, vol. viii. p. 39 (*b*) ; vol. ix. p. 31 (*b*) ; vol. x. p. 76 (*b*).) Hence "The Law presumes that they will do their duty" (Second Institute, p. 174).

13. These facts obviously bear, very importantly and instructively, upon the attempts which have lately been made, by the Justices in some counties in England, to interfere with and control the functions and the discharge of the duties of Coroners.

14. The Chapter in Magna Charta which declares that neither Sheriffs nor Coroners nor others shall hold [teneant] pleas of the Crown, does not in any way touch the foregoing function or position of the Coroner. It does not interfere with the power of Coroners to deal with [intromittere] Pleas of the Crown; nor does it affect the prohibition against the Sheriff's dealing with these without the Coroner. Appeals of felony, etc., etc., have, ever since Magna Charta, as well as before it, been constantly dealt with by Coroners;—while, on the other hand, it has always been settled that Justices of the Peace have no power to deal with several matters that fall within the functions of Coroners. Where a man had been indicted before Justices of the Peace, and, confessing the felony, had appealed others (that is, had turned approver, and made a formal charge against his comrades), it was adjudged by the Court of King's Bench that the proceedings were void, for that Justices of the Peace have no power to assign a Coroner to make the needful inquiry, and that Justices of the Peace have no power themselves to inquire touching the death of man, nor high treason, unless by special commission (Fitzherbert, Corone, 457 ; and see Coke's Reports, vol. x. p. 76 (b); Lambard's Eirenarcha, pp. 395, 409 [ed. 1614]; Rolls of Parliament, 7 & 8 Ed. IV. No. 20,—where it was refused to give the powers sought to Justices of the Peace). This point might be much further illustrated; but what has been now brought up is enough to show, in a very striking manner, the singular impropriety—not to speak now of the illegality—of the attempts that have been lately made by Justices of the Peace to usurp an authority over the proceedings of Coroners.

15. Eight years before what is called the Statute of Coroners, the Statute of Marlbridge (52 Hen. III.) contained an important reference to the functions of Coroners;—a reference

which will be found exactly to agree with the Common Law, as stated by writers earlier than the date of that Statute. It contains three distinct provisions: the *First* point is, that inquests ought to be held in cases of Robbery, Burning of Houses, etc.,—the fulfilment of which has latterly become neglected by Coroners, very much to the injury of public safety (compare before, Horne, par. 8). The *Second* point is, that all the inhabitants need not be present at inquests on Robberies, Burnings of Houses, etc.;—but that it will be enough if there be a jury sufficient in number to make a full inquiry (that is, twelve at the least): whereas in case of the death of man, none are to be excused attendance, except for good reason. The *Third* point is, that where the inquest finds death " per *infortunium*," it shall not be accounted Murder;—thus recognizing the full gravity of the responsibility attaching to the Inquiry before the Coroner. The last point has been already found alluded to by Britton, in another shape indeed, but resting on the same principle (par. 10).

16. The Statute of Westminster the first (3 Ed. I.) contains a clause as to the persons who ought to be chosen Coroners; which is important to the present subject, as further showing the nature of the functions belonging to the Office, the character of which is stated as the reason why men of marked sufficiency ought to be chosen to be Coroners. Their duty in regard to Pleas of the Crown (see above, par. 12) is insisted on; and the sheriffs are to be furnished with copies of the Coroners' Rolls,—an important security against loss or falsification, while the enactment itself involves the principle that the Coroners are the makers of the Rolls. To these are added a clause, to which special attention will hereafter be drawn, " that no coroner demand nor take anything of any man to do his office."

17. It was not till the year after the passing of the Statute of Westminster, that the Act commonly called the " Statute of Coroners" was passed. This fact, as well as the extracts from the writers on the Common Law already given, prove that the latter Act was not the origin of either the Office or

Functions of the Coroner, but that, unlike Justices of the Peace, who have no existence except a Statutory one, the Office and Functions of Coroners are part and parcel of the fundamental Institutions of England. The Statute of Coroners contains nothing new. The extracts already given show this. Its very terms show that it contains merely a recapitulation of some (but not all) of the heads of what was the preexisting Law on its subject-matter. The real meaning of the Statute was simply the same as attaches to very many other of the old Statutes, which, like it, are declaratory of the Common Law. It was a part of the very sound policy of the old practical system of our Institutions, that no man in England should be ignorant of any of the Laws and Institutions of his country. Some of the most important of these were therefore, from time to time, written out in a declaratory form; and, having been sanctioned by Parliament as correct—and so got put into the form of a Statute, they were then sent into every county in England, with the requisition upon the Sheriff to proclaim them in every city, town, and market-place within his county. (See Coke's Third Institute, p. 41, and Fourth Institute, p. 26; 'Local Self-Government,' pp. 135–139.) There could be few matters on which it was more important that this course should be taken than in what regarded the sacredness of human life. Hence the " Statute of Coroners " (4 Ed. I.).

18. The terms of this Statute do no more than follow what has already been quoted from the Books of the Common Law. The Coroner is declared to be under the *obligation* to hold an inquiry, whensoever he has Notice, either from a public officer or by private men of the neighbourhood, that any one has been *slain*, or has *suddenly died*, or has been wounded, or that a House has been broken, or that Treasure has been found. And it must be noted that the public officer here mentioned was a very different person from the Policeman of our day. He was the Constable or Head-man of the Parish, freely elected by the inhabitants. His nearest equivalent at the present day is the Churchwarden. This has been fully shown elsewhere (see 'The Parish,' *Second edition*, pp. 55, 68, 120). The Coroner is,

then, by this Statute declared to be bound to go immediately to the place where the body lies [statim accedere debent], and forthwith to summon a jury [et statim mandare debent, etc.]. He is not allowed any discretion,—any more than the Lord Chief Justice of the Queen's Bench has any discretion whether or not a writ shall go out of his Court, at the instance of any one demanding it. What puts the Coroner in motion is not any discretion of his own. His action proceeds, not from himself, but from the Notice he has received. It is not lawful for him to exercise, in any case, any discretion whatever in following up that notice. He is *bound* to hold an inquest when moved thereto by the receipt of a proper notice, whether this come from a local public officer, or from any private individuals, or from the keeper of a " prison " or other place of confinement.

19. It is remarkable that this " Statute of Coroners " repeats, twice over, the requisition that Inquests shall be held in every case of " Sudden death," as separate and distinguished from the deaths of persons " *slain.*" It also specifies deaths by drowning. Thus the same fact is here made prominent which the Books of the Common Law make equally prominent, namely, that the most important characteristic of the Coroner's duty, as regards the death of man, is, that he shall hold an Inquest in every case of "sudden death," without exception, and of death (as by drowning) under unknown circumstances. In the case of one palpably slain, the slayer would be charged : and the " appeal " against him would come before the Coroner in another department of his duties. But the great and all-important characteristic of the Coroner's Office, as to Inquests on Death, is, to ascertain, in cases *where there is nothing on the face of it to show that there is any circumstance that implies the suspicion of foul play,* and therefore no apparent ground of charge against any one, how every person who is unexpectedly found dead, or has died suddenly, has died, and who are the persons and what are the circumstances that can be shown to have stood in the nearest relation to the person thus dead. It is very remarkable that the sacredness of human life should have been thus surrounded with such safeguards

and solemn responsibilities, at the earliest period when our law assumes its definite shape; and it is far from satisfactory or creditable that it has been reserved for our own day to shake the safeguards which were, thus early, so carefully thrown around it.

20. The peculiar characteristics that have been thus pointed out as marking the Statute of Coroners, are further illustrated by the fact, that the same Statute does allude to the taking of "appeals" [charges] before the Coroner in some cases, while the Statute of Gloucester (6 Ed. I.) has further provisions for cases where the slayer of life, though not feloniously, shall stand charged of the deed. (See pars. 10, 15.)

21. The importance of the due fulfilment of the Coroner's Office in all cases of the death of man, is further recognized in the *Articuli super Cartas* (28 Ed. I. c. 3); the terms of which were repeated in 5 Ed. II. But the Statute of Exeter is the most important illustration of the subject which the Laws of England have kept on record for our instruction. The exact date of this Statute is uncertain, but it is assigned to the 13th or the 14th Ed. I.

22. The Statute of Exeter is an illustration of the means which the Constitutional System of England has always, until of late years, had in use, to ensure that those who have functions affecting the public welfare put into their charge, will fulfil those functions; namely, by a systematic and regular course of inquiry, and record of that inquiry, among those concerned (see 'The Parish,' pp. 35, 36). This Statute shows what the only supervision is which the Law of England has ever allowed to be held over the functions and action of Coroners; and thereby marks still more clearly the impropriety of the attempts lately made by certain Justices of the Peace.

23. The Statute of Exeter sets forth how inquiries ought to be made, touching the manner in which the Coroner "hath borne himself in his office." The Inquiry is to be made by a Body consisting of representatives chosen by every Town, Hamlet, and Parish in the County; as shown in 'The Parish' (second edition), pp. 35, 36. The Statute consists of two

parts: the one declaring the constitution of the Court of Inquiry; the other specifying the articles that are to be inquired of by this Court. Into the former, which strikingly contrasts with the position of Justices of the Peace,—who are neither chosen by, nor responsible to, the inhabitants of the Shires [see before, par.12, as to the ground of the credit given to the Coroner],—it is unnecessary to enter here. Further details will be found in the accessible reference above given. The latter is exceedingly remarkable, and puts the special duty of the Coroner, as to inquests on the death of man, in the same prominent and unmistakable position as has already been shown to be its right characteristic. The very first item in the Articles bound to be brought before the proper Court of Inquiry is, touching death by "accident" [aventure]. Murders, felonies, etc., follow,—but the "accidents" take the lead. (See before, pars. 8–10.) The Statute then goes on to declare that it is to be inquired:—"Whether the Coroner in his proper person went thither [to the place of the Body found] to do his duty, or sent another in his stead to do that which belonged to him to do. And, if he did so, how many times, and for how many accidents [aventures]. And who it was that went in his stead. *And if the Coroner went there willingly, without making delay or excuse, as soon as he was able, or not.* Or if he demanded anything, or his clerk took anything, for his hasting to do his office, or if he wilfully stayed back, for the sake of gain,—*after he had knowledge of the accident [aventure], upon being sent for."*

24. There is thus again forced upon attention the clearest view of what is the duty of the Coroner at Common Law. What has been already shown to be the Law, is seen to have had the strongest enforcement given to it; namely, that an inquest shall be held in every case of sudden death—sometimes called "aventure" and sometimes "misaventure," but the matters included within which have been already shown (pars. 8, 10) ; —and that the holding of such Inquest is the Coroner's primary and most important function.

25. The Statute of Exeter was no idle declaration. The

inquiries and presentments were, for centuries, regularly made in conformity with it. And the presentments thus made serve but further to illustrate what has been already said. Thus we find it presented that "a death by accident [aventure] was not found in the Coroner's roll [that is, he had held no inquest on it] ; and the Coroner was [therefore] adjudged to prison till he had paid a fine" (Fitzherbert: Coron. 292; and see ib. 183, and Hale, P. C. ii. p. 58). In another case, where the not holding of an inquest was no fault of the Coroner, because he had not had any notice given to him, it was presented "that a parish had buried a man who had *died suddenly*, and who had *died of a fever*, before he had been seen by the Coroner [*i.e.* without an Inquest] ; and the whole parish was [therefore] fined." (Fitzherbert: Coron. 329.) And it is laid down, as explicitly, by the Court in another case, that "those who *die suddenly* ought to be seen by the Coroner [*i.e.* to have an Inquest held thereon]." (Fitzherbert: Coron. 402.) It is rather a curious thing, and affords an instructive confirmation of the principle that is really involved, that, in Hale's 'Pleas of the Crown' (ii. p. 57), it is doubted whether the death in the case above named as from *fever*, was from fever or from hunger. In the original technical law phrase, the words when written bear some resemblance ["feyme" and "feivor"] ; but, if there be any mistake, there can be no real doubt that it is made by Hale, who only says that he had seen a *copy* of the document quoted, rather than in the second and carefully revised edition of Fitzherbert, which is quoted above. And Hale may be quoted against himself on this matter. (See after, par. 95.) But, however this may be, the case tells equally strongly against the late attempts of Justices of the Peace to interfere with the functions of the Coroners; for it has been already shown that Horne, writing long before either Fitzherbert or the record which he and Hale both refer to, puts, as illustrations of death by "aventure," that it is to be the very point of inquiry before the Coroner, *whether* it has happened through poverty [*i.e.* mere *hunger*] or through a *common pestilence* (before, par. 8); while Britton expressly illustrates the meaning of "aventure" by the case of one who dies by any *sudden malady* (before, par. 10).

26. That the regular course of Inquiries, in accordance with the Statute of Exeter, was kept in practice till after the passing of the Act 1 Hen. VIII. c. 7 (to be presently mentioned), is proved by the tractate on "The Offyce of Coroners" contained in the little work on "The Offyce of Shyryffes, etc.," published in the reign of Henry VIII., and which is one among the set of Treatises alluded to in the Preface to the tenth volume of Lord Coke's Reports, p. xviii (*b*).

27. The enactments in 14 Ed. III. (Stat. 1, c. 8) and 28 Ed. III. (c. 6) are no more than declaratory, and relate to the sufficiency of Coroners and the mode of their election,—matters, it must be said, which are too little understood and heeded in the present day.

28. The next Statute that relates to Coroners is one that has indirectly led,—through the misinterpretation of a later Statute which has grown out of it,—to the attempts of some Justices of the Peace to interfere with the functions of Coroners. To understand the Statute alluded to, it becomes necessary to consider a point which has, as yet, been only incidentally glanced at.

29. It is a common mistake to imagine and represent Coroners as having been originally entitled to no remuneration for their services. Instead of this, the true fact is, that Coroners were always entitled to remuneration, and always formerly received it ; but it was a fixed remuneration, and not one dependent on the number of Inquests taken,—to the due discharge of their duties as to which they were kept up by the Inquiries under the Statute of Exeter. .Coroners, like all other judicial functionaries, have always been deemed, by the Law, entitled to fitting remuneration ; though, like other Judges, they could not lawfully make any gain out of any individual case. A comparison of some Statutory declarations and other records will make this matter very plain.

30. It has been seen that, by the Statute of Westminster the first, it is declared " that no Coroner shall demand nor

c

take anything of any man for *doing his office.*" But these naked words must be interpreted by comparison with other Statutory declarations. Thus, in a later part of the same Statute of Westminster, it is said :—"No Sheriff, nor other King's Officer, shall take any reward for doing his office,— *but shall be paid by that which they take of the King.*" How entirely this applies to the case of Coroners will be obvious; but if authority is needed, Coke's Second Institute, p. 209, and Fitzherbert, Coron. 462, will be enough. The passage quoted from the Statute of Exeter completes the interpretation. The unlawfulness is there stated to consist in "demanding anything, or taking anything, for *hasting to do his Office,* or *wilfully staying back, for the sake of gain.*" What the Law forbade was, the making a special gain out of the individual occasions when need for the discharge of his functions arose ; but the Law has always recognized the right of the Coroner to remuneration from other sources. One, and a very considerable, item in the remuneration of every Coroner had, from early times, been, a fixed payment from every Parish, at every Circuit of the Justices in Eyre. The amount originally recognized as thus due, though the change of money-value has made it now seem trifling, was, in fact, a very considerable sum, and, coming from every parish, must have produced a handsome salary. This was "a right due to his office;" which is a very different thing from being incident to any individual discharge of its functions (Fitzherbert, Coron. 372 ; Staundford's Plees del Coron, p. 49; The Offyce of Coroners, as before, sig. k. iii. (*b*) ; Coke's Second Institute, pp. 176, 209, 210). Nor is this the only remuneration to which both Common and Statute Law recognize, from of old, the right of Coroners. It is enough now to illustrate the fact, without entering here on details, by referring to Rolls of Parliament, 2 Hen. IV. No. 74; 23 Hen. VI. No. 39; adding, that we have even proof that special levies were sometimes made for the sustentation of Coroners (Rolls : 35 Ed. I. Pet. 77).

31. The Statute which has led to these remarks, is the 3 Hen. VII. c. 2. It is a note-worthy fact, and one which bears

materially on the matter now in hand, that Lord Bacon, in speaking of this Statute, makes no allusion whatever to the Coroner's fee. It is plain that this was deemed a merely incidental provision in, and not the main point of, the Statute. The times, for the last few years—from the close of Ed. IV. to this year—had been disturbed and uneasy, and murders had increased. By the old Law, the wife or heir of a man killed might "appeal" (that is, prosecute) the slayer, as for a private wrong; and the indictment in the King's name could not be made, to the superseding of this, till a year and a day had passed. Hence much mischief had arisen. It was in consequence of this that, in this year, "There was made also another Law for peace in general, and repressing of murders and manslaughters, and was in amendment of the common laws of the realm; being this,—That whereas, by the common law, the *King's* suit, in ease of homicide, did expect [delay till the end of] the year and the day allowed to the *Party's* suit by way of appeal; and that it was found by experience that the Party was many times compounded with, and many times wearied with the suit, so that in the end such suit was let fall; and by that time the matter was in a manner forgotten, and thereby prosecution at the King's suit by indictment (which is ever best *flagrante crimine*) neglected; it was ordained that the suit by indictment might be taken as well at any time within the year and the day as after." (Lord Bacon's History of King Henry VII.)

32. It is self-evident that, as the finding of the Coroner's Jury constitutes, in itself, the indictment of him whom it records as guilty of the slaying, and as the persons who would give notice to the Coroner of the death of a man murdered, would usually be either the Parish constable (see before, par. 18) or the nearest relations, the same circumstances that had hindered indictments had also heretofore hindered the giving notice to the Coroner of the death. Hence it was that, in a Statute having what is so well put by Lord Bacon as its main object, the Coroners were naturally invoked to the full and prompt discharge of their known duties. And it is to be spe-

cially noted, that this Statute treats everything as resting with the Coroners; for, though Justices of the Peace are expressly named in the same Statute, the only power given to them is, that, if a known murderer escape, the " Justices of the Peace have power to inquire of such escape."

33. There is no implication in this Statute that the Coroners had been at all remiss in cases of death by *misadventure.* But it was foreseen that its passing would call for more of their time in the other class of cases. Unwisely therefore,—and departing herein from the wise rule so stringently laid down of old,—instead of securing and adding to the fixed salary and emoluments of the Office, it enacted that the Coroner should have a fee, in every case of every body slain or murdered, of 13*s.* 4*d.* out of the goods of the slayer, or out of the amerciaments levied upon the township for his escape. At the same time, a very heavy penalty was imposed upon the Coroner for neglecting to hold an Inquest.

34. It is quite certain that, at the time when the act last mentioned was passed, Inquests on deaths by *misadventure* were held with full regularity, and that its only object was to meet the other class of violent deaths. But that act had an unexpected though very natural effect. In offering a fee on a certain class of inquests, it naturally suggested the desire of a fee in cases of Misadventure also. To prevent the mischief hence arising, it became necessary to pass, a very few years afterwards, the Act 1 Hen. VIII. c. 7. This act is one of great importance to the matter in hand, for it affords direct and unanswerable proof, that the Statute Law hereon has had no other object but to recall and enforce the Common Law; and that the remedy of mischiefs sought by it was, to ensure the full carrying out of the Common Law, and not the making of any alteration in this. The Act recites the Act of Hen. VII.; and then adds :—" *Since which Statute* so made, the Coroners have used that, if any person hath happened to be slain by misadventure, and *not by no man's hand*, that they will not inquire upon the view of the Body so by misadventure slain, except they have for their labour 13*s.* 4*d.*; which is

contrary to the Common Law, and also to the Statute afore rehearsed." To restore the full action of the Common Law, therefore, the Statute "ordaineth that, *upon a request made to a Coroner to come and inquire upon the view of any person slain, drowned, or otherwise dead, by* MISADVENTURE, the said Coroner *diligently* do his office," under penalty for default.

35. It will be seen that this Act simply enforces the old Common Law, while it refers to cases of "misadventure" in a way which entirely agrees with the writers on the Common Law. And we happen to have incidental proof of the importance attached to this part of the duties of Coroners, in the language used, only a little later, by Sir Thomas Smith; who was himself Secretary of State to Edward VI. and Queen Elizabeth, and therefore speaks with peculiar knowledge of what was deemed, in the most authoritative quarters, the actual course of administrative duty. Speaking of the Coroner, he says:—"And if the person slain (slain I call here, whosoever he be, man, woman, or child, that violently cometh to his death, *whether it be by knife, poison, cord, drowning, burning, suffocation, or otherwise* [in the Latin edition it is "*alio quovis demum infortunio*"], be it by his *own fault or default,* or by any other); if, I say, the person slain be buried before the Coroner do come (which for the most part men dare not do), he doth cause the body to be taken up again, and to be searched; and upon the sight of the body so violently come to his death, he doth empanel an inquest of twelve men or more, of those which come next by, be they strangers or inhabitants; which, upon their oaths, and by the sight or view of the body, and by such informations as they can take, must search *how* the person slain *came to his death,* and *by whom* as the doer or cause thereof." (Commonwealth of England: book ii. chap. 24.) The Latin edition, which is in other respects also more precise and clear, has, in place of the last quoted words, the remarkable words—in the alternative— "*qua ratione tam lethale periculum defunctus adiverit; quis aut perpetraverit, aut modum facinoris subjecerit.*" And the last words of the same chapter give the sound reason why the

name "Coroner" pertains to this Officer,—"quoniam *cujusque subditi mors* ET *internecio* ad Coronam spectare intelligitur, etc.;" language which was no novelty, as the old Cases show (see Year Books, 29 Ed. III. pp. 41, 42).

36. That the Statute of Hen. VIII. was effectual in putting a stop to the misconception that had arisen out of the Statute of Hen. VII., and that the Common Law as to deaths by misadventure was thenceforth carried out without demur, might be fully illustrated. It is enough for the present purpose to refer to such well known authorities as Lambard (Eirenarcha, book iv. chap. 4, p. 434) and Dalton (Justice, pp. 226, 227, ed. 1622). The events which arose out of and followed the civil wars and final revolution of the seventeenth century, had the unhappy effect, of bringing into more or less of disuse that system of habitual Inquiries, which forms the characteristic method by which the spirit and practice of the English Constitution and its operative Institutions were maintained in efficient action. Nevertheless, it was two centuries and a half before there arose any such symptoms of want of the thorough fulfilment of the functions of Coroners, as to lead to any Legislative declarations on the subject. This fact is important. And it is exceedingly remarkable that when, after the lapse of that long space of time, Statute Law speaks again upon the subject, it is not with the slightest pretension to alter the old Law, but simply to re-enforce it. The source of the Salary of the Coroners had, meantime, almost died out, (apart from the great change in the value of money) through the unfortunate disuse of the system of those periodical Inquiries, at the holding of which it was that every Parish paid its contribution. The Salary of the Coroners had thus, by the operation of circumstances, shrunk almost to nothing, without any intention of the Law, and, in fact, contrary to that intention. Hence it became necessary to restore the remuneration to which they were entitled; and this was what was sought to be done by the Statute 25 Geo. II. c. 29. Unfortunately, the precedent taken, instead of being that of the Common Law, was that of the Statute of Hen. VII. But no alteration

was attempted to be made in the Law touching the holding of Inquests. On the contrary, the specific object of this Statute was, to enforce that Law, as it stood at Common Law, and had been already declared and enforced by many Statutes. And the language of Lord Coke may well be quoted here;— that "forasmuch as Acts of Parliaments are established with such gravity, wisdom, and universal consent of the whole realm, for the advancement of the commonwealth, they ought not, by any constrained construction, out of the general and ambiguous words of a subsequent Act, to be abrogated, but ought to be maintained and supported." (Reports, vol. xi. p. 63).

37. The words of 25 Geo. II. c. 29 are, however, not "ambiguous." The "constrained construction" that has, after the lapse of nearly 100 years, been attempted to be put upon them, gives an extraordinary example of the losing sight of every principle and rule that is best established in the Law and Policy of England, and in the construction of Statutes.

38. The Statute 25 Geo. II. c. 29 begins with the recital that "the office of coroner is a *very ancient and necessary office;*" thus explicitly declaring the importance of this office, in and with the characteristics and functions that have been shown to have always marked it. The Act goes on to recite the Statute of Hen. VII.; and adds to this recital, that the sums received under that Act are "*not an adequate reward* for the GENERAL execution of the said office,"—that is, in cases of inquisition on *misadventure,* etc. It has already been shown that this was so, and that neither the Common Law nor Statute Law ever contemplated that the fees arising under the Statute of Hen. VII. should form the remuneration for the *general* execution of the Office. The Statute proceeds :— "*To the intent, therefore,* that Coroners may be *encouraged to execute their office* with *diligence* and integrity, be it enacted," etc. (Compare the words at the close of par. 34.)

39. This Preamble puts the intention of the Statute beyond the possibility of real doubt, or of even tenable dispute. It proves that the latter was not framed with the remotest notion of giving any new powers to Justices of the Peace, but solely

with the object of ensuring the thorough discharge of the *"general"* duties of Coroners, by Inquests on *Misadventures* (as distinct from and beyond those on persons slain or murdered), in fulfilment of the functions of this *"very ancient and necessary* office." The mischief that existed, was not that Coroners had exceeded the duties of their office. On the contrary, the object of the Act was, that Coroners should be "encouraged to execute their office with diligence and integrity." The mischief was, that they now had "not an adequate reward." We have thus the most explicit specification of what the *intention* of the Act was, as well as of what the *mischief* was which the Act sought to remedy.

40. Had the principles of common sense alone, or those which have been laid down by the highest authorities as the only sound and guiding ones in the construction of every Statute, been followed, it would not have been possible that this Act should ever have been misinterpreted;—still less that it should have been distorted, and actually perverted to an exactly opposite meaning to its true one, as has, within the last few years, been attempted to be done by some Justices. "The good expositor," says Lord Coke, "makes every sentence have its operation to suppress all the mischiefs before the said Act, and chiefly those which are specified in the Act itself" (xi Reports, p. 34). "The original intent and meaning is to be observed; and the office of Judges is, always to make such construction as to suppress the mischief and advance the remedy, and to *suppress subtle inventions and evasions for the continuance of the mischief,* and *to add force and life to the cure and remedy,* according to the true intention of the makers of the Act, *pro bono publico"* (ib. p. 73, and before, par. 3). In the present case, it has, within a few years past, been sought, by "subtle inventions and evasions," not only to neutralize the Act altogether, but to give it a force that shall greatly increase the mischief, instead of suppressing it and advancing the remedy.

41. "The preamble," says Lord Coke in another place, "is to be considered, for it is the key to open the meaning of the

makers of the Act, and the mischiefs which they intend to remedy. . . . A man" must "consider in what point the mischief was before the Statute, and what thing the Parliament meant to redress by this. . . . Every Statute ought to be expounded according to the *intent* of them that made it, [even] where the words thereof are doubtful and uncertain, and according to the rehearsal of the Statute" (Fourth Institute, 330). In the present case, the words are neither doubtful nor uncertain.

42. The intent of the Act having been declared, it is enacted, " That *every inquisition*,—NOT taken upon the view of a body *dying in a gaol or prison*,—which, from and after the 24th of June, 1752, shall be *duly taken* (in England) by any coroner or coroners,—in any township or place *contributory to the rates* directed by an act made in the twelfth year of the reign of his present Majesty [Geo. II.], intituled, 'An Act for the more easy assessing, collecting, and levying of County Rates,'" etc. etc.

43. Before proceeding with the enacting words that follow, it is necessary to understand the precise meaning of the lines thus quoted. They contain the statement of three distinct *conditions* under which the enactment is to apply. *First :—* it must be an Inquisition *not* taken on one dying in *gaol or prison ; —second :—*it must be an Inquisition *" duly taken ;" —third :—*it must have been taken in a township or place that is *contributory to the County Rates.*

44. The *first* of these points will be more conveniently considered with reference to the second section of the Act. It is enough now to remark, that the second and third sections are specifically and separately directed to inquisitions on deaths in prison, and on bodies " slain or murdered,"—thus giving added force to what has been already pointed out as to the purpose and intent of the Act, in regard to the " general " execution of the Office.

45. The *second* point is very important. It has been much mystified, with a confusion of ideas and reasoning that is truly amazing, and only to be accounted for by the little

attention given to the history and bearings of this important subject (see before, par. 2). But the point is, in reality, transparently clear; and there cannot be a moment's real doubt as to what is the actual meaning of the language used in the Statute. It has been already shown, both by common and statute law, in *what manner* an Inquisition must be taken. Unless it be taken in that manner it is not "*duly taken.*"

To this " duly taking," there are five essentials.

46. The *first* of these essentials to the " duly taking " of an Inquisition is, that the Coroner shall have had Notice of the death, either by some public local officer (Parish Constable, Churchwarden, or the like), or by some inhabitants of the neighbourhood, or (in case of death under restraint) by the keeper of the place where one under restraint has died; and that, thereupon, he shall have summoned a jury. This formal Notice is of precisely the same nature, as regards the founding of proceedings, as is a writ or summons in any other Court; and it has been shown that the Coroner has no discretion whatever as to holding an inquest when such formal Notice has been put before him (pars. 7, 9, 10, 18). On the other hand, it has been shown that every place is liable to penalty, if the Coroner is not immediately certified of any death by violence or misadventure, as also is the keeper of any place of restraint, if he do not give the Coroner notice of every death within it. The withholding of Notice to the Coroner is, in fact, an indictable offence (1 Salkeld's Reports, p. 377; 7 Modern Reports, 10; and see Hale: Pleas of the Crown, i. p. 424; ii. ib. p. 57). The Coroner cannot himself with propriety act merely on his own original motion, though he is bound to prosecute every place and person which, having the duty to give him Notice of a death, has failed to do so. To what has been already said on this point, no more need be now added, than to quote the words of Chief Justice Holt:—
" The Coroner need not go *ex officio* to take the inquest, but *ought to be sent for* " (Salkeld's Reports, p. 377).

47. The *second* essential to the " due taking " of an Inquisition, is, that it shall be taken *upon view of the Body* of the

dead man;—which view must be had by both Coroner and Jury. If an Inquisition is pretended to be taken without a view of the Body, it is not "duly taken," and is absolutely void; the primary means to the ascertainment of how the dead man came by his death being thus wanting. (See before, pars. 7, 9; Fitzherbert: Corone, 107; Staundford: Plees del Coron, p. 51; Coke: Second Institute, p. 32; Hale: Pleas of the Crown, vol. ii. p. 58; Hawkins: Pleas of the Crown; book ii. ch. 9, s. 23; *R.* v. *Ferrand,* 3 Barnewall & Alderson's Reports, p. 261.) This primary point is of such obvious and fundamental importance, that it is thoroughly proper to disable the Coroner from receiving the remuneration attached to his office unless it be fulfilled. It is known that some Coroners have been so ill-informed, or so careless, as to have pretended to hold inquests without a view of the body having been first had by the Coroner and the Jury.

48. The *third* essential to the due taking of an inquisition is, that there shall be a jury of the neighbourhood, consisting of an indefinite number, but it must be twelve at the least;—a matter which has already been sufficiently illustrated (pars. 7, 10, 15, 35).

49. The *fourth* essential to the due taking of an inquisition is, that the record of it be signed by at least twelve of the Jurors, as well as by the Coroner (*R.* v. *Justices of Norfolk,* 1 Nolan, 141). It is unnecessary to enter into any detail upon the very obvious propriety of this requisition.

50. The *fifth* essential to the due taking of an inquisition is, that the record of it be complete and regular upon the face of it. If a material defect be visible on the face of the record, it is void; and, being the only record of the Inquisition, this proves the latter to have not been "*duly taken.*" Considering the high credit which, as already shown, is given to the Coroner's record (par. 12), this rule does but sustain the dignity and credit of the Court and Office. As examples of these "defects on the face of the record," it is sufficient now to refer to the cases, *in re Cully,* 5 Barnewall & Adolphus, 230; *in re Daws,* 8 Adolphus & Ellis, 936; and *R.* v. *Brownlow,* 11 ib. 119. See also 6 & 7 Vict. c. 83, *s.* 2.

51. It is plain that, unless the Inquisition has been, in all these respects, " duly taken," the Coroner has failed in the fulfilment of the duty of his office, and can therefore have no claim whatever to anything that may arise to himself as incidental to its fulfilment. It has already been shown that, when the Coroner has once had Notice of a death, he is bound to hold an Inquest, and has no discretion whatever in the matter,—all that he has to do being, to take care that the Inquisition thereupon is " duly taken," and that thus no incomplete investigation or record shall have been made on a matter so solemn as what touches the life and death of man. It is to be remarked—and this, as the sense of the word " duly " has been perverted in some late examples, is important—that Lord Coke uses the same word in precisely the same sense, when he speaks of the first essential to the making of an Election of a new Parliament being, that it be " *duly* made;" which, to prevent misapprehension, he gives also in the Latin—" *rite*"; —that is, according to regular form and lawful order, as distinguished from any circumstances touching the Electors ; which latter are equivalent, in the case of an Inquest, to the actual facts touching the Body (Second Institute, p. 169).

52. The *third* point in the above-quoted words of this Act, is one which has a peculiar significance. This Act proposed to throw a new charge, for Coroners' remuneration, on to the County Rate. The parishes had hitherto, in the two different manners already mentioned (pars. 30, 33) borne this charge directly. An Act had lately passed (12 Geo. II. c. 29) which, for the first time, established the existing system of County Rates. In older times, charges that it belonged to the Counties to meet, were deemed able and fitting to be imposed and assessed by the men of the Counties themselves who had to pay them, duly assembled in their lawful and regular constitutional assemblies. (See, for example, Statute of Westminster the first, c. 18 ; 23 Hen. VI. c. 10.) Politer times have magnanimously disregarded, altogether, the ancient English prejudice as to the connection between taxation and representation ; and the 12 Geo. II. c. 29, which is the Act cited

in the above quotation, gave unrestrained taxing powers to the non-representative and irresponsible Crown-appointed Justices of the Peace. A few places, owing to circumstances needless now to dwell on, did not come within the range of county taxation: so inquisitions taken within them were left, by this Act, to the same course as formerly.

53. But the Act of 12 Geo. II. c. 29 only authorized payments to be made by the Justices out of the county rates, to certain and specified "ends and purposes." Without an express fresh authorization by Statute, the Justices had no power to pay any fresh charge out of those rates; for, as already stated, the Justices, being the creations of Statute, have no power, either to do any act or to pay any money, except what is given them by the "express words" of some Statute.

54. The Statute 25 Geo. II. c. 29 proceeds to enact, that, for every inquisition coming within the above conditions, "the sum of twenty shillings, and for every mile which [the Coroner] shall be compelled to travel from the usual place of his or their abode to take such inquisition, the further sum of ninepence over and above the said sum of twenty shillings,— *shall be paid* to him or them out of any moneys arising from the rates before mentioned,—*by Order of* the Justices of the Peace in their general or quarter sessions assembled for the county, riding, division, or liberty where such inquisition shall have been taken, or the major part of them;—*which Order* the said Justices of the Peace so assembled, or the major part of them, are *hereby authorized and directed* to make."

55. These words, like those already commented on, raise three distinct points.

56. The *first* of these is, the creation of the new payments of twenty shillings for each inquisition, and ninepence a mile; which are, in point of fact, to be in lieu of the old salary attached to the office of Coroner. The payment of these sums is made imperative and obligatory, and it is not left to the caprice and discretion of those under whose control the county rate is placed. The words are, *"shall* be paid." (See par. 68.)

57. The *second* point touches the mode in which the pay-

ment is to be made, namely, by the simply Ministerial Act of those in whose hands the County Rate is placed. These being the Justices of the Peace, of course this Ministerial Act has to be done by them. They are to make an "Order" for the payment upon the proper officer. To the right understanding of this matter, it is necessary to recall the very terms of the Act 12 Geo. II. c. 29, which has been already shown (par. 52) to be the ground-point of the enactment before us. Section 6 of that Act, after requiring all High Constables to pay over all moneys received to the County Treasurers, enacts that these Treasurers shall "pay so much of the money in their hands, to such person and persons as the said Justices, at their respective General or Quarter Sessions, or the greater part of them then and there assembled, shall, *by their Orders*, from time to time direct and appoint, *for the uses and purposes of the said recited Acts*, and for any *other* uses and purposes to which the public stock of any County is or *shall be* applicable by law." The Justices had, therefore, no power to make any Order for any payment except such as was authorized, either by some foregoing Statute, or by some future one. Hence, no payment could be made out of the County Rates, except (1) by an *Order* of the Justices duly made, and (2) which had been *authorized* either by one of the Acts recited in 12 Geo. II. c. 29, or by a future Act. Hence the closing words of the section before us; which form, therefore, the third point to which attention is to be now called.

58. The *third* point gives the direct authority for the making of the Orders, which will thus fix a fresh charge upon the County Rates. These could not, as has been shown, have been charged with such payment without such direct statutory authorization. But the Statute not only gives the necessary *authorization*: it further *directs* that this Order *shall* be made. The words become imperative in this case, inasmuch as the sole "*intent*" of the Statute was to secure a payment, which it has already enacted "*shall be paid;*" and the words now referred to are merely the means through which the requisition of the Statute is to be carried out.

59. The Justices of the Peace are only mentioned at all in this enactment, because every payment out of the county rate has, under the modern Law, to be paid by orders issuing from them. No discretion whatever is given to them, to pay or not to pay. They are simply ministerial officers, whose duty it is to obey the Statute. The words of the Poor Law Act (43 Eliz. c. 2) are, that the Overseers shall act, and shall make rates, "*by and with the consent* of two or more justices of the peace;"—words which certainly do seem to imply some amount of discretion in the Justices. But the rule, that "express words" are necessary to give powers to Justices, is so clear and unswerving, that it has long since been settled that the words quoted give the Justices no discretion whatever; but that their Act of "allowance" under these words is purely ministerial; which, if they hesitate to fulfil, will be enforced by Mandamus, peremptory in the first instance (See 'The Parish,' pp. 150, 561). And notwithstanding the very strong words of 6 & 7 Wm. IV. c. 96, requiring the fulfilment of certain conditions in the Form of every rate, it has still been upheld that the Justices have no discretion whatever, but must sign the rate, however bad and irregular it may in fact be. (*Queen v. Earl of Yarborough*, 12 Adolphus & Ellis, 416.) In the face of these decisions, it is absolutely impossible for any intelligent man to contend, or for any court that would command the respect of rational men to hold, that any power of discretion can exist as to making the "order" for payment to Coroners under 25 Geo. II. c. 29. (See par. 68.)

60. No power whatever is given by this section to the Justices, to question or control the action of the Coroner, or to consider, in any way, the propriety of the cases in which Inquisitions have been held, or to exercise any "discretion" in the matter. Without "express words" giving that power, they cannot lawfully attempt to exercise it. There is not the trace of any such words, either express or implied, in this section.

61. The second section of the Statute 25 Geo. II. c. 29, relates to Inquisitions upon bodies dying in "gaol or prison." It is particularly noteworthy that this section uses identically

the same words as the first section, in reference to the necessity that the inquisition shall be "duly taken." This is absolutely conclusive as to the sense in which those words are used in the first section, were any subsidiary illustration of that sense needed. Though deaths in prison are not named in the Statute of Coroners (4 Ed. I. St. 2), it has been shown that that Statute was merely declaratory of the Common Law; and it has been also shown that the Common Law required inquests to be made on all persons who died under restraint. (See before, pars. 8, 9 ; and see Fitzherbert : Coron. 421 ; Hale : Pleas of the Crown, ii., p. 57). This requisition being invariable, the words "duly taken" remain equally applicable, in these cases as in every other, with regard to the regular taking of the inquest, according to the essentials already shown. But they would be simply unmeaning and utterly inapplicable, were the perverted sense admissible, which some Justices have lately attempted to give to the words "duly taken" in the first section. It is not the walls of a building, it must be always remembered, that constitute a prison. The governor, or any officer or servant who happens to die within the walls of a prison, does not "die in prison," nor become the subject of an Inquest. It is the being under *"restraint of liberty"* that constitutes being in prison, whether that restraint is exercised in a common sponging-house in Chancery Lane, or in a County Gaol, or in a Lunatic Asylum, or in a modern Workhouse for the Poor, Reformatory, etc. The common sense of this matter and the authorities upon it, are happily entirely at one upon this point, and leave no colour for doubt. (See Staundford, Plees del Coron, 30 (b); Coke upon Littleton, 260 (a) ; Hawkins : Pleas of the Crown, b. ii. c. 18, § 4.) It is worthy of remark, that the case in Fitzherbert, in which the unlawfulness is affirmed of burying any one who has died in prison, without a Coroner's Inquest, was not the case of a public gaol, but of restraint exercised by a private person. That case applies to every private asylum, or other place, where Lunatics or any others are kept under restraint, as well as to any public prison, asylum, workhouse, or the like. The end of the in-

quisition in such cases is, "that the public may be satisfied,
whether such persons came to their end by the common course
of nature, or by some unlawful violence, or unreasonable hard-
ships put on them by those *under whose power they were con-
fined*" (Hawkins: Pleas of the Crown, book ii. ch. 9, sec. 21;
and see before, pars. 8, 9).

62. The third section of 25 Geo. II. c. 29 reserves the
right of Coroners to the fee of 13s. 4d. on inquisitions upon
bodies "slain or murdered," as enacted by the Statute of
Henry VII.; thereby, as has been shown, adding to the illustration that the main object of the present Statute was, to
ensure that inquisitions should be taken on deaths other than
those of a man slain or murdered;—that is, in accordance with
the long-established functions of this "very ancient and necessary office," on deaths that are either "sudden" or by "misadventure."

63. It will not be useful to dwell now on the later Statutes
touching the Coroner's Inquisitions. None of these affects
the question now before us, which turns entirely upon the
construction of the first section of the Statute 25 Geo. II.
c. 29. It has been already shown what was the Common
Law with regard to the functions and duties of Coroners, in
relation to Inquisitions touching the death of man. It has
been shown that the sole object of the Statutes that have been
passed on the subject, from first to last, has been, to ensure
that those functions and duties shall be fulfilled; and that the
especial and most particular object that has always distinguished those Statutes has been, to have a care that Inquisitions on deaths by *misadventure* shall be unfailingly held.
The Common Law on the subject has been shown; the mischief that had grown up; the remedy for the mischief; and
the true reason of the remedy (see before par. 3). Thus the
Statute 25 Geo. II. c. 29 stands before us with transparent
clearness, and "the office of the judges," in the construction
and application of that Statute, is put beyond a doubt.

64. But, within a few years past, some Justices have sought
to evade this Statute, and, in place of fulfilling their own

D

duties under it, to pervert it to a meaning exactly the reverse of that which really belongs to it, so that, instead of the mischief being suppressed, it is not only attempted to be continued, but to be increased a hundredfold. And it is now alleged by these Justices that the Courts of Law have supported them in these "subtle inventions." If this were true, it would show that the Judges, instead of having "made such construction as shall suppress the mischief, and add force and life to the cure and remedy," have, in point of fact, done their best towards overturning an Act of Parliament.

65. Neither any Court nor any Judges can *make* any Law. Their function is, to *administer* the Law of the Land. Courts of Law are, of course, as liable to error as all other human institutions. If a case is not brought before a Court in its right aspects; if the actual bearings of it are either not brought before the Court at all, or are so brought before it that their relations cannot be seen; the Court will, almost inevitably, come to a wrong conclusion, and its decision will be an instance of a precedent to be avoided, instead of to be taken as an example. A wrong decision is, indeed, often as instructive as a right one; for the fallacies on which it rests become marks through which, the sources of error being thereby seen, the road to a right decision is helped and strengthened.

66. This applies to the recent cases that have been before the Courts touching the present matter. Nobody ever thought of raising the pretences now set up by some Justices, until a very few years ago. When raised, the grappling with the subject of course required an accurate knowledge of the history and fundamental principles of the Law connected with it, and careful research into the authorities upon it,—qualifications which are too seldom found in our day. It is impossible to read these Cases, without perceiving that neither of these qualifications has been shown, in the points and arguments that have been brought before the Courts. The latter have had to deal with most imperfect materials; and it is no wonder that the decisions have not, all of them, been in accordance with the Law. But the most singular matter is, that so imperfect

and ill-considered have been the materials put before the Courts, that it is the literal fact that no two of the recent decisions on this subject have agreed with one another. Hence the worthlessness of all stands demonstrated.

67. The older decisions are clear and consistent. According to these, it has been the Law of England from the earliest times, as it still is, that if a township bury a Body, whether slain or murdered, or suddenly dead, or dead by misadventure, before the Coroner be sent for, " the township shall be amerced ; and if the Coroner comes not to make his inquiry, upon Notice given, he shall be fined in Eyre, or in the King's Bench, or before the Justices of Gaol-delivery." (Hale : Pleas of the Crown, i. p. 424 ; ib. ii. p. 58 ; and see before, pars. 23, 25.) It has been fully shown, above, that the Justices of the Peace never had any jurisdiction or control whatever over the Coroners or their proceedings ; but that, on the contrary, the office of the Coroner is one whose jurisdiction has always been exclusive, and the credit of whose records is paramount (before, par. 12 ; and see ix. Coke's Reports, p. 119 (*b*)). It has been shown that the *presumption* of law is, that the functions of the office will be properly discharged ; and it is the unquestionable rule of Law, that whoever impeaches any incident of the discharge of such an office, is bound himself to prove the truth of his impeachment, and that the proof of right-doing cannot be thrown on to the Coroner. (See Preface to v. Reports, p. vii. (*b*); iv. Reports, 71 (*b*).) It has been shown that no jurisdiction or control whatever is given to the Justices by the Statute 25 Geo. II. c. 29 ; while it is very clear that such a conflict of jurisdiction as is thus assumed, would be of the greatest injury to the public interests, and could never have been proposed by any intelligent statesman, nor could it ever have been sanctioned by any intelligent legislature.

68. The case of the King against the Justices of Kent (11 East, p. 229) is often referred to, as a decision in which the Court of King's Bench affirmed the existence of the irresponsible authority now attempted to be assumed by certain Justices. Instead of this being the fact, however, that case

distinctly affirms the duty of the Court of Queen's Bench to interfere, on Mandamus, whenever the Coroner shows that he has fulfilled his duty, and that the Justices have not fulfilled the requisition of the Act of 25 Geo. II. c. 29. The case was one where the Inquisition had not been " duly taken " (before, par. 51). In such case, the Coroner was plainly not entitled to the fee. In the same way as the Justices, though compellable by Mandamus to sign a rate-book, cannot be asked nor compelled to sign a blank sheet of paper, under the pretence that it is a rate-book, but the Overseer must, on applying to the Court for a Mandamus, aver that a *bonâ fide* intended rate-book was presented for signature; so, the Justices cannot be asked or compelled to make an " order " for payment of the Coroner's fee, unless the record is before them, which shows that the inquisition was " duly taken." If, on the face of it, the record shows that the inquisition was not " duly taken," the Justices have not the *power* to make any order for payment. If, on the other hand, the record shows, on the face of it, that the inquisition has been " duly taken " (see before, par. 43), the Justices have no power whatever to look at the *subject-matter* of the Inquest, or to enter into any consideration of the propriety of holding it. Those matters are for a higher Court, and the Law has thoroughly provided for their consideration, should they arise. The duty of the Justices is simply ministerial, namely, to make the " order ' in discharge of the Statute. (See par. 59.)

69. In the case of *R.* v. *Kent*, the Coroner had, after regular notice to him of one death, summoned a jury in due course of Law; and an inquisition was " duly taken " on that case; the fee for which, the Justices ordered to be paid, as they were bound to do. But, while on the spot, the Coroner was told,—not by any local officer or by independent neighbours, but by some of the Jury,—tha another man had died suddenly. Instead of waiting till he had proper Notice, and thereupon summoning a special jury for the case, as he was bound to have done, the coroner *re-swore the same jury*. This was altogether irregular, and a course liable to very great

abuse. The record thus plainly disclosed the fact, that the Inquisition was not "duly taken." The Justices therefore did not make any "order;" and they were right in not doing so. The Court of King's Bench in this case simply upheld the Law, that an Inquisition not "duly taken" does not impose on the Justices the obligation to make an "order." The meaning of the Court was made plain by the language used. Lord Ellenborough very properly declared that, for Coroners to "obtrude themselves" is "highly illegal." No doubt of it. This is no more than another way of putting what Chief Justice Holt has been already quoted as saying (before, par. 46), that they "ought to be *sent for*." And so Chief Justice Hale:—"*When* Notice is given to the coroner, of a Misadventure, *he is to issue* a precept to the constable to return a competent number of good and lawful men of the township, viz. twelve at least, *to make an inquisition* touching that matter." (Pleas of the Crown, ii. p. 59.) The functions of the Coroner must, like those of the judicial Head of any other Court, be *set in motion* from without,—not of his own action. Even if a Coroner sees a case that he thinks needs an inquest, his utmost course is, to point it out to the local authorities or neighbours, and await their requisition upon him, before he himself moves in the exercise of his office : but he must prosecute them if they fail (before, par. 46). In the above case, the Court was obviously quite right to decide, that they "did not see any occasion to interfere with the judgment of the Justices [namely, that, upon the face of the record, the Inquisition had not been "duly taken"] *in this instance*." The very terms of this decision, involve the assertion of the duty of the Court to "interfere" in other instances, where the state of facts is different, and where, an inquisition having been "duly taken," the justices have refused to make their order.

70. There is nothing, therefore, in the case of *R. v. Kent*, that helps those who wish to make out, that the Court of Queen's Bench has sanctioned the recent attempts at assuming a control over the Coroners, which have been made by some Justices. The case really tells in exactly the opposite way.

71. The above case is thus, in fact, quite in accordance with that of *R. v. Ferrand* (3 Barnewall and Alderson, p. 261); and equally antagonistic with the latter to any such attempts of the Justices. In the case of *R. v. Ferrand*, Chief Justice Abbot says:—"It is laid down by my Lord Hale, that, 'when it happens that any person comes to an unnatural death, the township shall give Notice thereof to the Coroner. Otherwise, if the body be interred before he come, the township shall be amerced.'" He then himself goes on:*—"*When* this notice is given to the Coroner, *his duty is* to issue a precept to the constable, to return a competent number of good and lawful men to appear before him to make an inquisition." There is no question of discretion, of discussing propriety or impropriety, and making out a foregone conclusion, instead of holding an inquisition. The Coroner, who is a judicial officer, cannot usurp the place of the jury, and presume to consider whether or not an Inquest ought to be held,—any more than Lord Campbell, before a writ is issued in his name, can take upon himself to say whether or not the plaintiff is in the right, and, if he fancies he is not, stop the proceedings. The Coroner is bound, when lawfully and regularly put in motion by a Notice of Death, to exercise his office;—all that concerns him being, to take care that the inquisition thereupon is "duly taken."

72. Mr. Justice Bayly, in the same case, remarked that—" The words of the Statute De Officio Coronatoris are *very emphatical; 'ad occisos accedant, vel ad subito mortuos.'* "

73. A case of the King against the Justices of Norfolk is also often referred to; which is alluded to (but not reported) in East's Pleas of the Crown, p. 382, but is fully reported in Nolan's Cases relating to the duties of Justices of the Peace, p. 141. This case can only have been cited, in support of the recent pretensions set up by some justices, either in ignorance

---

* The *substance*, but not the *exact words*, of what is thus quoted as from Hale, is found in ii. Pleas of the Crown, pp. 57, 58, but not at the place referred to by the Reporters. It seems better, therefore, to give, above, the words which the Reporters state to have been used by C. J. Abbott.

of the original Report, or on the assumption that the latter would never be consulted. It does not give the shadow of support to the pretensions of the Justices, while it confirms and sustains what has above been shown to be the Law upon the subject. It was a case in which four inquisitions had been pretended to be taken, in respect of which the Justices refused to make an "order" for the fee. When it came before the Court of King's Bench, it appeared that, upon the face of the pretended Inquisitions themselves, they had obviously not been "duly taken," for they were only signed by the Coroner and the Foremen of the Juries, instead of by twelve of the jurymen,—a practice illegal in itself, and as obviously dangerous as it is illegal (before, pars. 15, 49). The pretended inquisitions were "no inquisitions at all," and of course the Court refused to interfere. A point was attempted to be raised, as to whether inquests should be taken on bodies cast on shore ; but this the Court declined to enter on,—the point above named being conclusive. And not the slightest encouragement is given by this case to the notion, that the Justices have any discretion and control over the Coroners.

74. The next case is that of the Queen against the Great Western Railway Company, which arose in 1842 (3 Queen's Bench Reports, p. 333). But this was a case as to the *territorial jurisdiction* of a particular Coroner. Even that point was not well discussed in it, nor were all the authorities upon it brought forward and considered. The case is not, therefore, entitled to much weight, even upon the ground raised in it. But it was not a case that turned in any way upon the ordinary exercise of *functions.* Any observations made in the course of it on the latter subject, were, therefore, entirely extra-judicial, and can in no way compromise the Court. Part of what is said there, as reported, is, however, so extraordinary, and so plainly and directly in contradiction to the whole course of the Common as well as Statute Law,—while no authority is even suggested in support of it,—that it is necessary, out of respect to the Court, to infer that the note of the case was imperfectly taken, and that it has been printed with a trans-

position of negatives and affirmatives that has made the case a startling example of the fallibility to which single Reports of decisions are liable. It is put forth in the printed report, as having been said by Lord Denman, that " if, *in the course of evidence*, it should appear that *no murder or manslaughter is suspected*, the Coroner must *stop the proceedings and discharge the Jury*" !! How such a dictum should have crept into the report, it is impossible to say. It is not Law. It puts forth a proposition so preposterous in itself that it is not worth while even to enter on the disproof of it. Every child knows that it is the jury, and not the coroner, that has to say whether suspicion attaches to any one in any case; and that this cannot be known till all the evidence has been heard. A Turkish Cadi may " stop proceedings." An English Court has to hear them till the end. And, as the authority of Lord Chief Justice Hale is at least as sound as that of Lord Denman, it is enough to put, against alleged dicta so preposterous, the deliberate and careful words of Lord Hale:—" The jury is to be sworn and charged to *inquire*, upon the view of the body, *how the party came by his death;—whether* by murder by any person, *or* by misfortune, or as *felo de se*," (Pleas of the Crown, ii. p. 60 : and see further, below, par. 95). Happily, the Report of the judgment in this case of *R.* v. *The Great Western Railway Company* is inconsistent with itself, as the very next page to that which contains the above grotesque distortion of the Judges' dicta, makes the judgment speak of a verdict "*per infortunium.*" This case assuredly gives no help to the usurpations of the Justices.*

75. The next case is that of the Queen against the Justices

* With reference to this case, it must, moreover, be noticed, that it was discussed, and judgment was given, entirely as if it arose upon the Act 2 & 3 Edw. IV. c. 24; while that Act had been expressly *repealed* fifteen years before the case arose (7 Geo. IV. c. 64) !! Yet the Court of Queen's Bench was utterly unconscious of this fact; and this, although that very Act, 7 Geo. IV. c. 64 (§ 12), is cited in the judgment itself!! (p. 337.) This further shows, very strikingly, how little such cases as these have really been considered before and by the Courts, with an actual regard to and knowledge of the Law; and, therefore, how little authority anything that is said in them can really carry with it.

of Devon, and occurred in 1846. This case, which did not arise till nearly one hundred years after the Statute of 25 Geo. II. c. 29, was the first in which the attempts of the Justices (heretofore undreamed of) to control the functions of the Coroners, came before the Courts; and in this case the Court of Queen's Bench, after argument, *granted the Mandamus*, as prayed, against the Justices; and the Justices, instead of venturing to make any return to the Mandamus, thereupon paid the fees.

76. The case of the Queen against the Justices of Carmarthenshire occured the next year. And in this case, as if to show how little consideration had been given to the subject, both in the argument and in framing the judgment, the decision of the same Court, on precisely the same points, in the preceeding year, is not even referred to! Starting with such a glaring omission, the judgment in this case does not even touch upon the matters which have already been shown to be absolutely essential to the consideration of this subject. The two cases of *R. v. Kent* and *R. v. Norfolk* are referred to; but, instead of their true points being cited, they are treated as if illustrating points which do not even arise in them, and which are not in any way considered or adjudged in them;— and it is plain that the only full report of *R. v. Norfolk* (that by Nolan) cannot have been looked at by the framer of this judgment. What is meant by "duly taking" an inquisition, is not even considered. Out of premises thus erroneous, and with considerations thus overpassed, a conclusion is come to, for which no authority is given, and which is not only, in itself, contrary to the uniform current of all the judgments on this and the related subjects, and contrary to the undisputed Law for centuries, but the putting forth of which is in violation of the well-established rule of Law and of common reason, that Justices of the Peace, the creations of Statute, can exercise no powers "unless authority be given to them for such purpose in express words" (Hawkins: Pleas of the Crown, book ii. c. 8, s. 38; Hale: Pleas of the Crown, ii. 42, 43; Croke's Reports (Eliz.), p. 87; Strange's Reports, p. 1256;

Salkeld's Reports, p. 680; 3 Term Reports, p. 279; and see pars. 67, 96). It is, then, plainly not a true utterance of the Law when it is said,—avowedly as the result of an indirect inferential conclusion only (founded upon false premises and erroneous references to authority),—that Justices have a discretion in the execution of the Act of Geo. II., and that they can control the Coroner, and that they are irresponsible in that control.

77. This decision was in the teeth of the decision of the same Court in the preceding year. It was against law; and it cannot do anything to alter the Law. That it was against Law has been so fully shown already, that it is unnecessary to enter, as might readily be done, into a minute examination of it. If necessary, the proof that the case is not Law is capable of an exhaustive demonstration.

78. There were thus now two recent decisions of the same Court, in diametrical opposition to one another on exactly the same point; while the latter of them (*R. v. Carmarthenshire*) was in diametrical opposition, also, to every principle of Law, and to every previous decision on every related point that was, either nearly or remotely, involved in it.

79. In 1857, arose the case of the Queen against the Justices of Gloucestershire. Again, unhappily, the actual questions and principles involved, were altogether omitted to be brought before the Court, as had already been the case in *R. v. Carmarthenshire*. Again without materials for a sound decision, it is not surprising that the actual decision did not contain an exposition of the Law. But it is, on the other hand, very remarkable that, in this case, the Court drew back from part of what had been adjudged, by the same Court, in the case of *R. v. Carmarthenshire*; and that it granted the mandamus for one fee (that of 6s. 8d. under 7 Wm. IV. & 1 Vict. c. 68), which, as well as the fee under 25 Geo. II. c. 29, had been refused in that case. Thus, however, does the inconclusiveness and ill-considered character of both these decisions stand but the more plainly self-demonstrated. But the reason given for the departure, in this case, from the decision in

R. v. *Carmarthenshire,* is very noteworthy. It was said, and repeated over and over again, in the course of the discussion on the case (the short-hand writer's notes are here referred to), that " in the argument [of *R.* v. *Carmarthenshire*] there does not seem to have been any distinction made there " (Lord Campbell) ;—" the question was never raised there " (Counsel) ;—" if the distinction had been relied upon, it might perhaps have led the Court to think there was a good deal of doubt about it " (Mr. Justice Coleridge) ;—" you see that point was not raised as a separate point " (Lord Campbell) ; etc. etc. This related to the point above-said, in which this case overruled that of *R.* v. *Carmarthenshire.* Such language, which is heard every day in the Courts of Law, contains the recognition of a Principle which is of far greater importance than the incidental decision that happens to be arrived at ;—namely, that no Court of Law in England is bound by a decision, unless all the points, illustrations, and authorities, have been put fully before it. It is not, therefore, and it never can be, an imputation upon any Court, if a decision given upon imperfect materials or argument is overruled, in the same or any other Court, at a future time. The case of *R.* v. *Carmarthenshire* rested upon no data. No actual materials seem to have been brought before the Court ; and none of the true merits and principles involved were argued, or illustrated by the so richly abounding authorities. The decision in that case, far from being given with the intention of being antagonistic to foregoing decisions, went on the assumption that it was, on a fresh subject, in conformity with all that was brought before the Court. It has been proved, in the present Paper, that this assumption was an erroneous one. Already, when, on a later day, one single point was really raised before the Court, has the same Court overruled part of its decision in that case. It is not possible, consistently with the respect due to the Courts of Law, to doubt but that, if the other and more important actual points and principles which touch this subject had been properly brought before the Court, and fairly considered there, the remainder of the judgment in *R.* v. *Car-*

marthenshire would have shared no other fate than the part overruled in *R.* v. *Gloucestershire* has already done. The actual Law would have been again affirmed. Many cases of this kind have happened; and such cases inspire confidence, instead of distrust, in the Courts of Law. One of these gives an illustration that is singularly parallel to the present case; for the question was, like the present, one arising out of usurped jurisdiction. The usurpation was wholly confirmed by the King's Bench in one case (as in *R.* v. *Carmarthenshire*);—then it was partially shaken (as in *R.* v. *Gloucestershire*);—and, finally, it was wholly overthrown. (See Strange's Reports, pp. 776, 942, 1108.)

80. But, though those who desire that the attempts of the Justices at a usurped control over the Coroners should be sustained, have been thus shown to be unable to rest upon any course of consistent decisions in the Courts of Law, it is quite certain that, in making these attempts, the Justices are not only seeking to override the Law of the land on the special matter, but they are directly violating the first principles of the general administration of justice; principles which, while they are as old as the Law of England, and have been affirmed and reaffirmed for centuries in every possible way, happen also to have been embraced within decisions of the Court of Queen's Bench itself in several very recent cases. In the case of the Queen against the Justices of Surrey (November, 1855), a rule to quash an order made by the Justices, was made absolute, on the express ground that one of the Justices was interested; though he was only one of a number who had made the order, and though his only "interest" in the case was, that it was a rehearing of a case which he had already decided. (And see Hawkins: Pleas of the Crown, book ii. ch. 8, secs. 69, 70.)

81. Lord Campbell said, in the case last cited, that "it is of the last importance that the administration of Justice should be pure and above suspicion. It is only recently that the House of Lords reversed a decision of Lord Chancellor Cottenham, upon the ground that he had an interest in the subject-matter of his decision, although that interest was so in-

finitesimally small that no one could suppose it would have the most remote influence on his decision. . . . It would be most inconvenient if magistrates interested could act." And in a later case (*Dixon* v. *Earl of Wilton*, Feb. 1859), the same learned Judge well remarked:—"Such is the weakness of human nature, that those who sit as judges should not have a shadow of interest in the matter." Many other cases to the point might be cited. The rule is universal. But Justices have the control over all Prisons and Reformatories, over all county Lunatic Asylums, and—as *ex officio* Guardians of the Poor— over Workhouses. It has been seen to be the duty of the Coroner to hold inquests on all deaths within all of these places of confinement. The question of "interest" arises, then, directly. The inquisition is taken for the purpose of satisfying the public that there has been no mismanagement in the establishment where the death has happened. The Justices are, in fact, on their trial, in every such case, before the Court of the Coroner. And in some cases, as in the memorable one at Birmingham in 1853, it is only through the inquisition thus taken before the Coroner's Court, that abuses which have grown up, either through the Justices having directly permitted them, or not having been energetic enough in the fulfilment of their duties, have been disclosed to the world, and so put an end to. In all cases, it is the certainty of an inquest, that holds a constant wholesome check over mismanagement and abuse. There is, then, plainly no case in which the "interest" of the Justices is clearer or more direct. And if it were to be tolerated that those who are thus interested in the results of a large class of Coroner's inquests, shall be allowed to usurp a control over the "general execution of the said office" (which is what is grasped at under the misconstruction of 25 Geo. II. c. 29), justice would be scandalized, and the administration of the Law become a mockery. Where would be found the Coroner who, however anxious to do right, would be able to fulfil his duties in respect to this class of inquisitions, with integrity and impartiality? The Justices would be able to put the screw upon those who have to sit in judgment upon their own conduct. This point alone is enough to dispose for ever of the pretensions of the Justices. Added to what has been already said, it shows that, from whatever point of view this matter be looked at, the attempts that have been made by some Justices are altogether unsustainable, and involve a violation of the fundamental principles of the Law of England, as well as of common right.

82. And when the illustrations which Justices have given in various counties, of the exercise of that "discretion" and control which they are so eager to grasp, are looked at, it would seem indeed as if a judicial blindness had led them to pursue a course that demonstrates to all the world their entire unfitness for the exercise of that "discretion" and control which, in defiance of the Law of England, they have, in those cases, usurped. It is deplorable to think that any men who are entrusted with functions that can only exist for the public benefit, should be capable of the course that has been pursued; and should be found ready, for the sake of exalting their own importance, to attempt the enforcement of proceedings which are hostile to the plainest interests of the Public and to the common safety and welfare of Society.

83. It is not necessary, in order to show that this language in fact but faintly represents the spirit in which the Justices have proceeded, to do more than quote a few passages from the Report of a Committee of the Middlesex Justices, appointed on 17th October, 1850, and made to the April Quarter Sessions, 1851. In this Report, it is deliberately proposed to abolish the Coroner's Court entirely; to do away with the institution of the Jury; and to invest the Crown-appointed and irresponsible Justices with all the powers and jurisdiction of the Coroner's Court. It is difficult to say whether the ignorance or the self-sufficiency displayed in the following passage is the most conspicuous :—" It will be seen," says this Report, "that all the observations which have been made, tend to support the recommendation, *which your Committee now make*, of a *transfer to the Magistracy*—who already inquire, concurrently with the Coroner, into the more serious

cases within the latter's jurisdiction [*a statement which is wholly untrue*]—of the *exclusive cognizance of the whole.*" (Report, p. 29.) That a body of English Gentlemen should be found capable of deliberately making a proposition of this nature, the main point of which rests on an untruth, for the sake of increasing their own authority and importance, is sufficiently humiliating. But, to prevent mistake, we find this Committee explicitly declaring,—after referring to certain *ex parte* witnesses who, of course, "*condemn the use of Juries at Inquests ;*—and *in this view your Committee have no hesitation in concurring.*" (Report, p. 25.)

84. Profoundly ignorant of the Laws, in the administration of which they are appointed, within their proper sphere, to help, these Middlesex Justices do not even know the difference between an Inquiry and a Charge. They are unable to understand that the certainty of an investigation as to how every unexpected death has happened, is a far more effectual way of stopping experiments at foul play, than is the taking evidence against a murderer *after you have caught him.* Justice requires the latter : the common good of Society is best secured by the former. The function of Justices of the Peace is, to hear charges made against individuals for the positive commission of crimes and misdemeanours. The totally different function of Coroners is, to carry out an *inquiry* as to *how* and by what means every death has happened which, whether suspicion of foul play exist or not, is not in the ordinary course of nature ;—whether such death be by (1) slaying or murder, (2) any sudden or unexpected death, (3) any misadventure. (See pars. 7–11, 19, 23, 35, 74, 90.)

85. In conformity with the enlightened spirit thus manifested by the Middlesex Justices, that body has gratified itself by continually refusing to make the "orders" which it was bound at Law to make, for payment of the fees upon inquisitions which the Coroners have had no choice but to have taken before them, and which were, in every respect, "duly taken." Without enumerating a multitude of cases that have occurred from year to year, it is enough to say that, on 4th

April, 1859, these Justices refused to make these "orders" in the cases of inquisitions held upon the death of a child aged three years, found dead in the ruins of a fire ; of a child aged thirteen months, who died a violent death by scalding ; of a child aged twelve years, who died of severe injuries from burning ; of a child aged three years, who died from scalding, and whose mother did not call in medical aid ; of a child aged ten months, found dead in the ruins of a fire ; of another child aged four years, found dead in the ruins of a fire ; of a child aged six months, with cause of death unknown, but to whom no medical attendance was called till after death ; of a child aged seventeen months, scalded to death ; and of another child, aged nineteen months, who also died of scalds. Now every one of these instances was the case of a violent or sudden death ; and it does so happen that there is not one of them which does not come, not only within the spirit but, within the direct letter of the law requiring the Coroner to hold an Inquest ;—as has been already fully proved in the foregoing pages. Yet the Middlesex Justices picked out these cases (the only ones that even their caprice could alight upon, out of 187), in order to assert their superiority to the Law of England ; and they refused to allow the Coroner's fees on the inquests in those cases, on the pretext that inquests in them were unnecessary. If unnecessary in such cases, was there ever a case in which an inquest was necessary ? The young, the helpless, need the protection of the Law more than any. It is the certainty that no sudden or violent death can happen without a thorough inquiry, that operates as the surest restraint upon many who have infant life in their hands. Child-murders, for the sake of burial fees, are but too well known to have happened. It is no more than holding out a premium upon murder, when difficulties are thus attempted to be thrown in the way of the holding of Coroners' Inquests in such cases. The pretence of a desire to promote the Public Health, is a farce and a delusion, while Justices are allowed to give it out, in many counties in England, that, so far as they can, they will prevent the Law having its course, and will put a stop to any questions being asked in ugly cases. But for this, Palmer's crimes would not have had their opportunity.

86. We find not only the Justices of Middlesex showing the disregard for infant life which the cases just quoted demonstrate, but that the Justices of the West Riding of Yorkshire have encouraged and sanctioned the Chief Constable of the Police under their control, in the issue of what is pompously put forth as a "General Order;" in which the Instruction is coolly given, that "The Coroner should not be called in or informed in cases of *mere accidental death*, such as death caused by falling from a horse, falling from a scaffold at a building, *infants overlaid in bed, and such like*, where there is no suspicion of foul play, etc." That is to say, the Justices assume to themselves the power of making laws to override both the Common and Statute Law of England. It is difficult to deal gravely with proceedings of this sort. But they are too much fraught with danger to be made a jest of. They show an incapacity to comprehend the first principles of Law and administration and common sense, no less than a disregard for the safety of society.

87. Unhappily, several hundreds of instances might be cited, in which the Justices in some counties have thus unlawfully interfered with the due course of law. The position of Coroners anxious to fulfil their duty, has been made most painful. They have been compelled, in self-defence, to hold back from that discharge of their "very ancient and necessary office" which the Stat. of 25 Geo. II. c. 29 was passed for the express purpose of encouraging them in the diligent fulfilment of. The public safety and interests have thus become most gravely compromised. It is even a known and avowed fact, that one most competent to fill the office, and certain of election, declined to become a Candidate at the late election of a county Coroner for Middlesex, on account of the unseemly squabbles that have arisen through these unlawful attempts of the Justices.

88. It is noticeable, that the Justices have used the authority

E

which they have newly acquired over the county Police, to endeavour to accomplish the object of interfering with and controlling the action of the Coroners. They forbid these men to give the necessary Notices to the Coroners,—accompanying this with the implied assumption that no one else can give them. But this, again, only illustrates the ignorance which the whole course of these Justices displays. It has already been shown that policemen are not the proper persons to give these Notices. It is the independent and responsible local officers, or any respectable neighbours there, who are the proper persons to give the Notice, where the death has not happened in confinement (before, par. 18.)

89. The utter recklessness of the Law of the land shown by some Justices, is well exemplified by a resolution passed by the Justices of Norfolk at the Quarter Sessions in January, 1858: —" That every coroner acting in the county, should require a certificate from a magistrate, clergyman, or guardian, instead of churchwardens and overseers as heretofore."* There is something intensely ludicrous in these Magisterial exhibitions of legislative cravings. They are very much like the impotent positiveness of a spoiled child or a wilful girl. The Law of England happens to be, that notice of death may be given to the Coroner by any local officer or by any honest men of the neighbourhood ; and upon such notice he is bound to act. Such resolutions as the above, prove their authors' ignorance of or contempt for the Law, and their determination to attempt the usurpation of an authority which the Law has never dreamed of giving them. They are, of course, unlawful and

* The Justices of Suffolk have, since this was written, gone even beyond their brethren of Norfolk. On the 1st July, 1859, a Committee of Justices recommended to the Court of Quarter Sessions, and the latter adopted the recommendation, "that the duty of summoning Coroners be imposed upon the Police Constables of the County," instead of being the duty of the Local Authorities. It appears, from the Report of the Committee, that this recommendation was adopted at the instigation of General Cartwright, one of the Government Police Inspectors. So much for the progress of Centralization in England.

It is needless, after what has been before shown, to enter into proof that the Justices have not the slightest power either to make such a recommendation, or to adopt it. The Coroners will act unlawfully if they give heed to it.

wholly futile ;—*but the public does not know this: and so they are too often successful.* And they show the position to which the Justices, in some counties, are systematically endeavouring to reduce the " very ancient and necessary office " of Coroner ;—namely, to one of subserviency and dependence, instead of independence ; until, as seen in the modest recommendation of the Middlesex Justices, the Office is altogether abolished, and its functions,—without the incumbrance of a jury to be satisfied,—are handed over to the irresponsible Justices themselves.

90. One form in which the Justices have often interfered, where they have not gone to the extravagant lengths above exemplified, is by resolving,—as the county of Southampton did at the Michaelmas Sessions, 1857,—" That no inquest ought to be held upon a dead body, except when *the Coroner has received information,* affording reasonable ground for *supposing* that the death has been occasioned by some criminal act or culpable neglect." How entirely illegal and worthless such a resolution is, has already been proved. But it were impossible to illustrate the want of power of logical perception more forcibly than such a resolution does. It proves the inability of such men to comprehend the difference between an *inquiry* and a *charge;* a difference which even the history of the Coroner's functions would have so aptly illustrated, had the nature of that office been studied, instead of being only attacked (before, pars. 14, 19, 84). The object of an inquiry is to *get information.* It is asserted by these wise Justices that you are not to *seek* information, unless you have got it beforehand. You are only to *inquire,* if you have already arrived at a foregone conclusion. (This subject has been fully considered in ' The Parish,' second edition, pp. 374–379.) The Coroner, as a judicial officer, can have no " information," except of the fact of the death. He can have no " suspicion," until the Jury have given their verdict. It is the Jury before whom information is to be laid, and who alone are to be the judges whether or not there is ground of suspicion against any one. It is the Public, and not the Coroner, whose place it is, in all cases, to

be satisfied. In order that the Public shall be satisfied, they must know that there has been no hole-and-corner secret *exparte* chattering and earwigging, but that there has been an open public inquiry, where the truth has been searched out in broad day, before the full Coroner's Court, " whither all persons may resort, and in no chambers or other private places." (Second Institute, p. 103.) It is, unhappily, a known fact, that some Coroners have so far forgotten the duties of their office, and their own personal self-respect, that they have actually degraded themselves by accepting from the Justices the payment of a fee for *not* holding an inquest;—thus at the same time pandering to the Justices' desire to supersede the office, and proving their own disregard of their oath of office, and of all their actual functions. It need hardly be said that such a course is justifiable under no Law, either Common or Statute, but that the offering and acceptance of such moneys is a high crime and misdemeanour, alike in the Coroner who accepts it and in the Justices who pay it. The office of the Coroner is, to summon a jury of free men to make an inquisition as to the cause of the death of one who has died. He has no power to forejudge the decision of that Jury;—still less to have the presumption to supersede it, by obtruding his own opinions in the place of the Verdict of the Jury. It is the Jury, and the Jury alone, who have to come to conclusions upon the evidence before them. The Coroner has to take care that their inquisition is " duly taken." No more insidious attempt at undermining the fundamental Institutions and Principles of the Law can be made, than when, for their own purposes, a body of irresponsible functionaries induce a public officer to be recreant to his duties, and to be instrumental in setting aside the fair and open inquiry by free men into facts that touch the safety of individuals and the well-being of the public.

91. It should be remarked that the Act 7 & 8 Vict., c. 92, § 21, affords no justification or shelter for the practice last-named.

92. Careful as our fathers were of the sacredness of human life, it is amazing that, in our day, when the subtlety of man

has discovered so many methods of destroying life unknown in simpler ages, and when professions of regard for the poor, and for the security of the public health (which must be supposed to include *life*) are on every one's lips, this new crusade should have been raised against an Office whose peculiar function it is, to have care taken that *no man dies the death whose life is unaccounted for*. Those who are most intimate with the abodes and the wants of the poor, are most sensible of the unspeakable value and importance of the due discharge of this office. "It has always been held," says one of the Medical Officers of London (1 March, 1859), " that the office of Coroner, who is elected by the people, and therefore is independent of the government, and who is aided by a jury, is one of the most efficient means we possess for the protection of life, and as a safeguard against oppression. *It is impossible to over-estimate the importance of securing a thorough administration of this office.*" "The true object," the same writer correctly observes, " of a Coroner's Inquest is, to ascertain the '*cause of death;*' and thereby *either* to satisfy the community that *no wrong* has been done to the deceased, *or* to lead to the bringing the criminal to justice, if wrong has been done." It is strange and lamentable that there should be any men in England, holding the Commission of the Peace, who are unable to comprehend a proposition so plain, but so important, as what is thus stated ;—a proposition which, as has been shown, is in strict accordance with the whole spirit and practice of the Law of England on this subject.

93. The defects in the administration of the Law of Scotland, arising from there being now no functionary there fulfilling the duties of Coroner, and from all cases of unexplained deaths being there left in pretty much the same case as they would be in England were the modest proposition of the Middlesex Justices carried out, is well known to those who are familiar with the intimate domestic history of Scotland. Some considerations on this subject, with startling but very instructive illustrations, are stated in a paper lately published by Mr. James Craig (Edinburgh, 1855).

94. It must be distinctly understood, that there is no point which has been touched upon in this Paper which might not have been more fully considered, and strengthened with even further proof. Should the rash endeavour be made to contradict those primary authorities on the Law of England who are here taken as the guide, there will be no hesitation in meeting, and no difficulty in disposing of, the quixotic adventurer who shall essay so hopeless an errand.

95. To conclude :—Not only was life held sacred in the older times in England, but, even in the time of Lord Chief Justice Hale, it was laid down, by that distinguished Judge himself (whom, *pace* the authors of such decisions and dicta as we find in *R. v. Carmarthenshire* and *R. v. Gloucestershire*, it may still perhaps be allowed for Englishmen to hold in some respect), that those open and vulgar methods which are commonly called murder and manslaughter, are by no means the only dangers that exist to human life. "There are," says that great Judge, " several ways of killing : (1) By exposing a sick or weak person or infant unto the cold, to the intent to destroy him, whereof he dieth. (2) By laying an impotent person abroad, so that he may be exposed to and receive mortal harm ;—as laying an infant in an orchard, and covering it with leaves, whereby a kite strikes it, and kills it. (3) By imprisoning a man so strictly that he dies. (4) By starving or famine. (5) By wounding or blows. (6) By poisoning. (7) By laying noisome and poisonous filth at a man's door, to the intent by a poisonous air to poison him. (8) By strangling or suffocation." (Pleas of the Crown, vol. i. p. 431.) And the same great Judge,—not being able to foresee the possibility of such forgetfulness of the Law of England being found in any decisions in an English Court of Law as is found in the published Reports of *R. v. Carmarthenshire* or *R. v. Gloucestershire*,—elsewhere says :—" Now sudden violent deaths, which ARE ALL *within the Coroner's office to inquire*, are of these kinds :—(1) *Ex visitatione Dei* [this being here, as in the Statute of Exeter, put first in the list,—and being illustrated by the same Judge when he says, " *Contagious diseases*, as

plague, pestilential fevers, small-pox, etc., are common among mankind *by the visitation of God*" (vol. i. p. 432 : and compare before, par. 25, as to Inquests on deaths by fever)] ; (2) *Per infortunium*, where no other had a hand in it,—as if a man falls from a house or cart; (3) By his own hand, as *felo de se* ; (4) By the hand of another man, where the offender is not known ; (5) By the hand of another, where he is known, whether by murder, manslaughter, *se defendendo*, or *per infortunium.*" (Pleas of the Crown, ii. p. 62 ; and compare ib. i. p. 418.) Every one of these cases, and every other akin to them,—so many of which have already been illustrated by the authorities that have been quoted in this Paper on the subject of "misadventure,"—has to be investigated before the Coroner's jury. That *each and all* should be thoroughly investigated, in every case, is what the Law of England has always required, and now requires. This is the great protection which Society has, against the multiform shapes which crime against human life is known to take. The *certainty* of the inquiry being made in every case of sudden or unaccounted-for death, is the only sure restraint on crime. The childish attempt to stop inquiries, unless a foregone *suspicion* can be raised,—an attempt which shows an ignorance of that principle of English Law which holds every man innocent until proved guilty,—is nothing more than an encouragement to crime, and a premium upon those abhorrent applications of science to the purposes of crime, of which but too many examples have been disclosed within late years. By the Law of England, the *abatement* of the cause of death follows the verdict of the Coroner's Jury that death has been so caused. (Fitzherbert, 416; Hale, Pleas of the Crown, i. pp. 431, 432 ; ii. p. 62; Hawkins: Pleas of the Crown, iii. p. 111 ; before, par. 10.) The question of "suspicion" against an individual, cannot have any place here.

96. The duty of the Coroner is now the same as it has always been. The safety of man's life and the welfare of Society, need the exercise of his functions at least as much in modern times as they have ever done before. On notice of

a death, violent, sudden, or resulting from misadventure, or happening to one who is in confinement, it is the Coroner's bounden duty forthwith to summon a jury, and to make inquisition, on view of the body (external and internal), as to the " cause of the death." Formerly, a sufficient salary recompensed the arduous and highly responsible labours of this "very ancient and necessary office." Now, the Coroner is entitled to the less satisfactory remuneration of a fixed fee on each case in which the record shows that the Inquisition has been " duly taken." The Justices of the Peace have the Ministerial duty of making an " order " for the payment of this fee ;* but they have no discretion whatever to question or control the exercise by the Coroner of his functions. When they make an attempt so unlawful, it were well that they should be reminded of the words of Lambard—for so long ago did these Crown-appointed functionaries seek to encroach beyond their actual and lawful sphere of duties—when he declares (p. 58) that " Truly it is to be wished, That Justices of the Peace would not, by colour of the reference to their discretion in some *few* cases, arrogate unto themselves authority to use their discretion, and to play (as it were) the Chancellors, in *every* cause that cometh before them. For no way better shall the discretion of a Justice of the Peace appear, than if he (remembering that he is *lex loquens*) do *contain himself within the lists of law*, and (being soberly wise) do not use his own discretion but only where both the law permitteth and the present case requireth it."

TOULMIN SMITH.

8, *Serjeants' Inn* (*E. C.*), *June*, 1859.

---

* In 1803, a Bill was before Parliament for increasing the mileage fixed by 25 Geo. II. c. 29. It was lost, after passing through several stages and divisions, by only the narrow majority of *five*.